Crunch Munch

JONATHAN LONDON

Illustrations by
MICHAEL REX

Silver Whistle

Harcourt, Inc.

San Diego   New York   London

Printed in Hong Kong

Animals like to eat,
and so do you.
Some nibble,
some gulp.
Some chomp,
some chew!

How does a beaver eat?

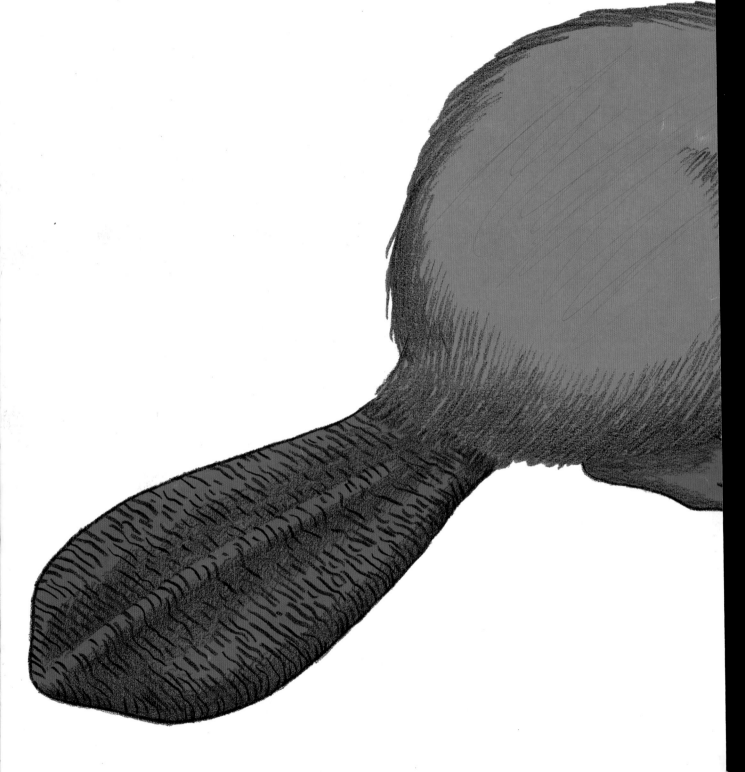

CRUNCH *munch,*
CRUNCH *munch*

How does a cow eat?

MOO-O-O-O chew, MOO-O-O-O chew.

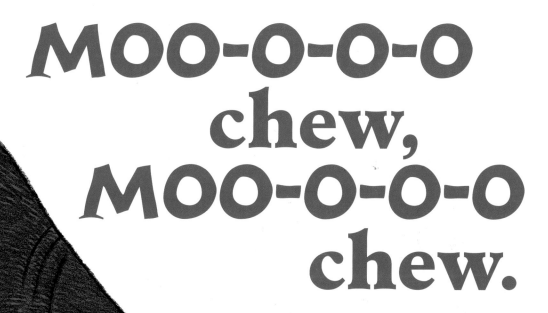

How does a chipmunk eat?

Nibble bibble,

nibble
bibble.

How does a frog eat?

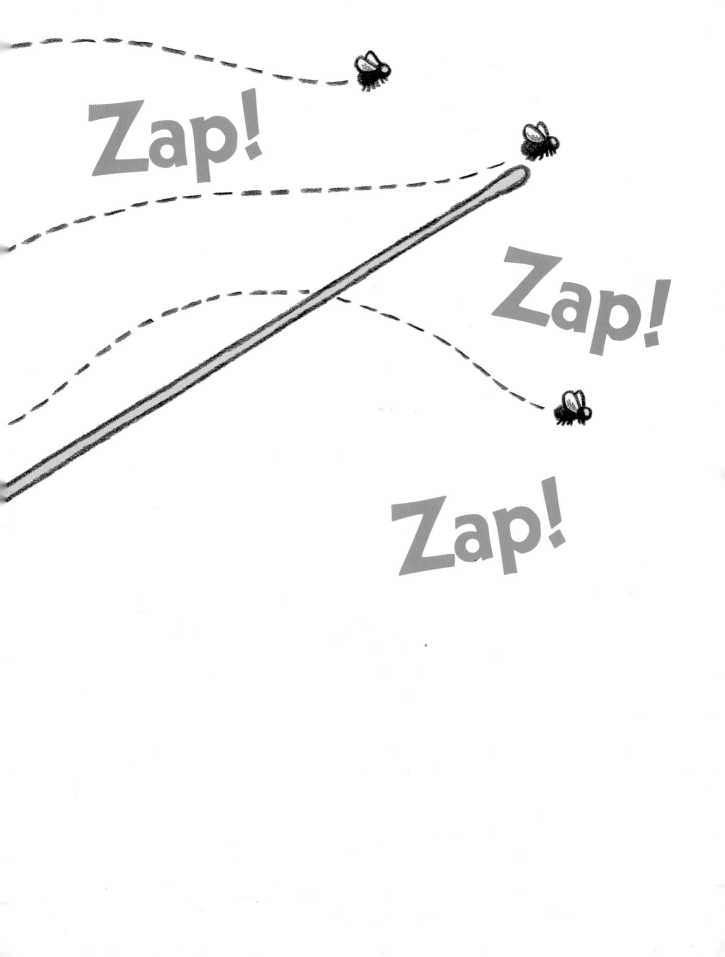

How does a pig eat?

Slop, slop, slop.

How does a bear eat?

GRUM,
GRUM,
GRUM.

How does a giraffe eat?

**RIP-scrunch,
RIP-scrunch.**

Lippity-lap, lippity-lap.

How does an aardvark eat?

Sluuurp–GULP,

Sluuurp-GULP.

How does a woodpecker eat?

Peck, peck, peck.

Now all together, let's crunch, munch, nibble, and scrunch!

CRUNCH munch,
CRUNCH munch,
goes the beaver.

MOO-O-O-O
chew,
MOO-O-O-O
chew,
goes
the cow.

Nibble bibble,
nibble bibble,
goes the chipmunk.

Zap!
Zap!
Zap!
goes the frog.

Slop, slop, slop, goes the pig.

GRUM, GRUM, GRUM, goes the bear.

RIP-scrunch,
RIP-scrunch,
goes the giraffe.

**Lippity-lap,
lippity-lap,**
goes the cat.

Sluuurp–GULP,

**sluuurp–
GULP,**

goes the aardvark.

Peck,
peck,
peck,

goes the
woodpecker.

Now take a seat.
How do *you* eat?

For Sean, Max, Jeff, and Leah, and all kids who like to eat
—J. L.

To Gregory, who is just beginning to crunch and munch
—M. R.

Requests for permission to make copies of any part of the work should be mailed to the following address:
Permissions Department, Harcourt, Inc., 6277 Sea Harbor Drive, Orlando, Florida 32887-6777.

www.harcourt.com

Silver Whistle is a trademark of Harcourt, Inc., registered in
the United States of America and/or other jurisdictions.

Library of Congress Cataloging-in-Publication Data
London, Jonathan, 1947–
Crunch munch/Jonathan London; illustrated by Michael Rex.
p. cm.
Summary: A rhythmic description of the different ways in which
various animals eat, from a frog eating flies to a cat lapping milk.
1. Animals—Food—Juvenile fiction. [1. Animals—Food habits—Fiction. 2. Food habits—Fiction.]
I. Rex, Michael, ill. II. Title.
PZ10.3.L5834Cr 2001
[E]—dc21 00-9144
ISBN 0-15-202603-7

First edition
A C E G H F D B

The illustrations in this book were done in colored pencil.
The coloring was done with Adobe Graphic Software.
The display type was set in Victoria Casual.
The text type was set in Sabon.
Printed by South China Printing Company, Ltd., Hong Kong
This book was printed on totally chlorine-free Nymolla Matte Art paper.
Production supervision by Sandra Grebenar and Pascha Gerlinger
Designed by Lydia D'moch